A Cat who Became American

*Immigrant cat named Kinoko,
a true story…*

**Texts and Illustrations
MARIE UEDA
www.marie-ueda.com**

Copyright © 2021 by Marie Ueda

All rights reserved. No part of this publication may be reproduced, distributed, or transmitted in any form or by any means, including photocopying, recording, or other electronic or mechanical methods, without the prior written permission of the publisher, except in the case brief quotations embodied in critical reviews and other noncommercial uses permitted by copyright law.

ISBN: 978-1-63945-286-6 (Paperback)
         978-1-63945-215-6 (E-book)

The views expressed in this book are solely those of the author and do not necessarily reflect the views of the publisher, and the publisher hereby disclaims any responsibility for them.

Writers' Branding
1800-608-6550
www.writersbranding.com
orders@writersbranding.com

for all cat lovers everywhere.

Introduction
My family portrait

My name is Kinoko. I was born on the 12th of February, 1975 in Lisbon, Portugal. My mother was white; I never knew my father. I was born out-of-wedlock and raised by my single mother. I had one brother who was also white; he had patchy black spots on his body, but I was somehow born entirely black, including my whiskers. My mother gave birth to us in a kitchen. As a Portuguese cat who ended up in the United States is a long story: it was a dramatic tale of my life as a cat.

At the time I was born, Portugal was under the uprising (1974-76) - 500 years old colonialism ended and a dictatorship government fell, and Portuguese people were struggling to create a democratic state – it was also known to the world *The Flower Revolution or Carnation Revolution*, because on the day of Revolution, on the 25th of April, 1974, not even one shot was fired and instead, the Portuguese people were giving red carnations to soldiers with tanks on the streets for a symbol of peace. In retrospect, it was one of the most remarkable political transformations in the twentieth century old European history.

During the uprising, in the city of Lisbon there were no tourists - instead, it was filled with foreign diplomats, CIA agents, espionage, spies and journalists. Among them were a couple of an English journalist and a Japanese photojournalist. They were both foreign correspondents reporting on the revolution for *The Guardian* newspaper of London. Both dearly loved cats and were looking for a kitten to adopt. They put a notice on a bulletin board in a neighborhood supermarket, announcing: *"KITTEN WANTED — calico, tabby, white, black, ginger, or any other kind. Please call us if you have any of them."* A Portuguese housewife, an owner of my mother, saw the notice and contacted the couple. By then, I was about seven weeks old.

When I turned eight weeks old, we had a visitor. The Japanese woman named Marie came to interview me and my brother. She picked up both of us together, holding us in her hands examining our faces. Then, all of a sudden, because we were tiny and fragile, we slipped out of her hands and fell down to the floor. My brother yelled, "MEOW!" very loudly. "Oh, no! I'm sorry!", she quickly apologized. It did hurt me too, but I didn't meow. Because I didn't complain or scream, Marie instinctively thought that I could become a healthy and strong cat, and decided to take me home. Before she took me away, my mother's owner explained to Marie how I should be fed. In Portugal at that time, cat food was a luxury item and only for Portuguese fat-cat's cats. The woman told her that most Portuguese cats are raised on human food: meat, fish, cheese and milk.

Next, she put me in a cardboard box and I was carried by Marie to her home. When we got to her apartment on the fifth floor of a residential building, a man was waiting at the door and greeted me with a big smile. His name was Chris, Marie's partner, the journalist. This is how I was adopted by a foreign couple. Marie became my human-mother and Chris was my human-father. Thus my new life had begun with them; this was the beginning of the long story of my life as a cat.

Episode One
Meaning of Kinoko

When I first started to leave my cardboard box, I was barely able to walk, instead, I wobbled. Out of curiosity, I looked around the apartment. I felt that everything was very big and tall except me. I was the only tiny creature in there. I became scared and wanted to hide. As I lurched across the floor, I discovered a kitchen. I saw a narrow gap between the stove and the wall, which was the perfect place to squeeze into, and warm too. For the first few days, I just sat in that space.

Marie called to me to come out of there, but so far I had no name. For days, she and Chris talked about naming me, discussing what to call me. Watching me in the dark, Marie told Chris, "This kitten is like a *Kinoko,* because he is growing up in the dark (Kinoko means mushroom in Japanese)." "Well, let's call him Kinoko, then!" he answered. That's how I got my name. It sounded odd to Japanese who rarely call their cats after vegetables, but not to others. Chris thought it sounded rather charming in English. This is how I became Kinoko and I've been called Kinoko ever since.

Episode Two
In the Kitchen

I could run faster and faster each day. After a few more weeks, I was jumping up and down off of chairs, sofas, beds, and back up onto tables. Like all kittens, I played with anything that moved. I was playing well and eating well. I became a very healthy kitty eating human food.

As I grew bigger, Marie changed my menu to accommodate my growing size. She used ingredients that were good for growing cats; she became my personal chef. Choosing from my favorite food, she created her own special recipes. My dish usually held white fish, chicken or meat boiled up with white rice to which added vegetables like green peas, carrots, sweet corns, potatoes or beans etc., in something that looked like porridge. She cooked this in a large pot twice a week and kept it in the freezer until feeding times. I ate my "porridge" twice a day, morning and evening. Marie created a special gourmet menu just for me at that time. For this reason, ever since I was very young, I have known what humans eat - they eat the same food as I do.

Episode Three
Onion Fume

The kitchen was the best place for me to hang around, because it was where my food was cooked and where I was fed. Because I was still tiny, Marie allowed me to do anything I wanted. She never got mad at me even when I jumped on the kitchen counter or table.

One time she was chopping up some vegetable on the counter. Out of curiosity, I jumped up. I just wanted to find out what she was doing, thinking that perhaps she was cooking my meal. As I examined what she was chopping, I got tears in my eyes. The more closely I looked, the more tears ran down my face. So, I had to rub my eyes with my paws.

Then, Marie called out to Chris saying, "Kinoko is crying because I'm chopping onions!" Both of them looked at me in tears and laughed at me! I wondered, and at that moment I couldn't figure out why I had tears streaming from my eyes, and Marie didn't. Later I learned that she was wearing contact lenses in her eyes and that I wasn't.

Episode Four
Paper-balls

Because he was a journalist, Chris worked until late hours in the night typing articles for The Guardian. The sound of typing in the living room often kept me awake. Out of my cat-curiosity, I always hung around him in order to see what he was doing. Once when I was watching, he grabbed the paper he was typing, made it into a ball and threw it on to the floor.

So, I began playing with the paper as a football, running with it and pushing it all over the room. I was very excited by the crispy sound of the paper as I played. While I was doing this, more balls kept coming one after another. And very soon there were paper-balls all over the floor. Then, it crossed my mind that perhaps he needed the paper-balls back later. So I began fetching them in my mouth and bringing them back to him one by one. This is how I learned to fetch things and bring them back to Chris and to Marie as well. It was just an accident. To be honest, I wasn't trying to be a dog! I never knew until later that this is something dogs do for their masters.

Episode Five
Kinoko gets a nickname

Chris had an interesting talent: he was good at drawing. As he worked at home, I hung around him on his desk all the time, and I soon became his best friend. We developed a kind of special relationship, the kind that happens to many writers and their cats.

His other companion, as he worked, was a glass of wine — his favorite drinks were Portuguese green wine called *vinho verde* or Portuguese beer. After a few drinks, he became a very good cartoonist - the more he drank the better he drew. One morning when I woke up, I found drawings of pussycats in the living room. When I examined them closely, I realized they were all portraits of my face drawn with four different expressions. Each of them was named *"Poogle," "Woogle," "Choogle,"* and *"Noogle*. I thought he should be a cartoonist rather than a journalist. They were so real that I felt that I was looking at my own face in a mirror. After that morning I was nicknamed *"Poogle-Woogle-Choogle-Noogle."* It was such a long name that they decided to call me simply *"Pugo"* from *Poogle*.

Episode Six
Adolescent

When I became three months old, I found myself with a strange excitement. Marie used to do the laundry each week. After finishing the washing, she sorted out the bed sheets, underwear, clothes, etc., and then ironed them in the kitchen. While I was watching her doing this, I used to play with the laundry, rolling over inside and out of the piles of clean clothes.

One day, as usual, while I was playing with the cleaned laundry, all of a sudden I wanted to make a pee, so I did it on the clean clothes. Marie watched me doing this and screamed, "What are you doing, Kinoko?" But it was too late. The clean sheets were already wet. After I did this, I felt so good; it was the most exciting feeling that I had ever had. After that, I did the same thing repeatedly. Marie got angry at me, because she had to wash it again, complaining, "You're such a naughty boy!" But I couldn't explain myself to her.

Marie and Chris called their cat-lover friend to get advice on what could be done to stop my behavior. He explained to them that any male cat who reached adolescence might do such a thing for "sexual pleasure." Now they had learned something new: I was not a kitten anymore. I had become an adolescent — I had reached the human age of 13 years old!

Episode Seven
In the cat clinic

Marie and Chris decided that it was time to have me neutered. I was taken to a neighborhood cat clinic by Marie. In my country, no appointment was necessary at animal clinics, not like in America. When we arrived at the clinic, there were nearly 15 cats in the waiting room. They were sitting on their owners' laps. It was the first time for me to meet other kitties and I became very excited. There were all kinds of cats in the waiting room: ginger, calico, tabby, white, gray, long hair, short hair, fancy cats, handsome cats, ugly cats, and black cat like me.

When I looked at them out of curiosity, they looked back at me. We began communicating through our eyes, asking each other, "Where do you live?" "What kind of food are you eating?" "Is your family nice to you?" Most of them responded that they were happy with their Portuguese families, but they wanted to meet other cats occasionally in order to have kitty-buddy community.

So, while I was there, I formed a pussycat party naming it *The Portuguese Cat Party* (its abbreviation was PCP). Under the revolution, Portuguese people had formed all sorts of political parties, so why not for cats? I thought we should also have "cat-rights" too, just in case we needed them.

Episode Eight
Operation

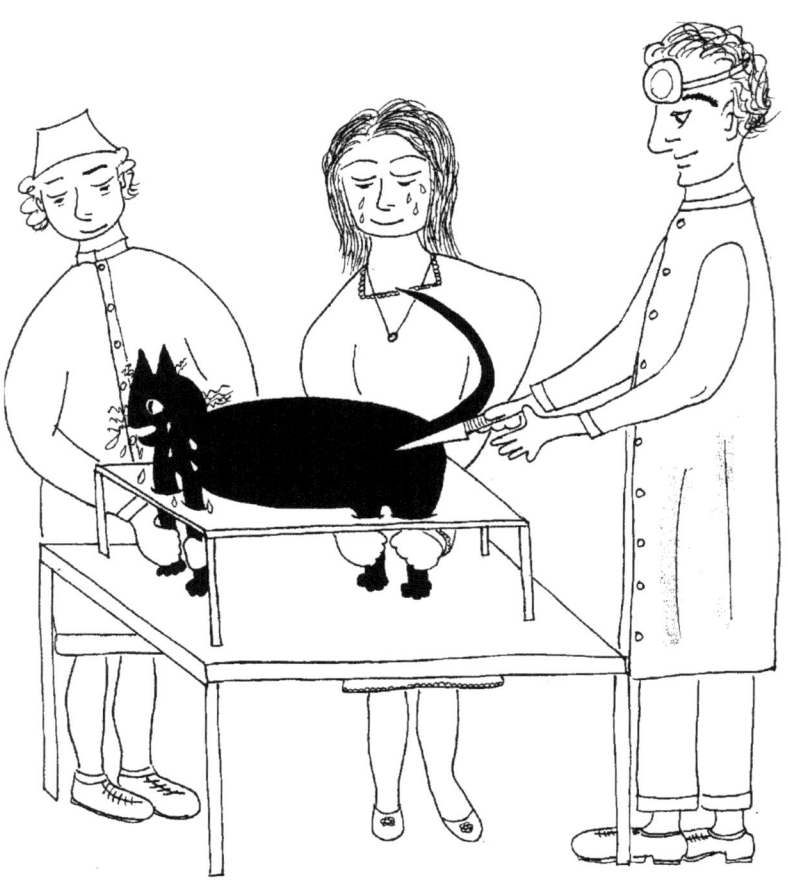

My name was called. I was accompanied by Marie to the doctors' room. To begin with, I couldn't understand why I had to be there, because I wasn't sick. In the center of the room there was a tiny table with four holes, which had been placed upon the operating bed. A nurse quickly took hold of me and laid me on top of the table, placing each of my legs through one of the four holes. The next moment, a doctor appeared with a surgical knife in his hand. I instinctively knew what he was going to do to me: he had come to cut my "thing" out. There was no way for me to escape because my four legs were stuck in the holes. Then, the doctor began his business straight away, without giving me any "anesthetics".

When a sharp knife entered my body from the back, I SCREAMED, "MEOW!!!" As I was screaming in pain, the nurse and Marie grabbed my paws so tightly that I couldn't move. I WAS SCREAMING, SCREAMING, SCREAMING!!! GIAOOO!!! "This is a cat-abuse!!!" GIAOOO!!! "We need cat-rights activists right now!!!" GIAOOO!!! "Please someone, stop this barbarism!!!"

Marie was so shocked by this cruel procedure that she was in tears. It lasted only one minute but it seemed to me hours of horror. My country at that time was poor, and anesthesia was only used for humans, not for animals as we were regarded as "third-class citizen"; we didn't have any cat-rights, we badly needed them after the revolution. I was glad that I had just formed the "PCP" for the sake of Portugal's future cat generations. Anyway, the operation was successful and I didn't die at least. The cost of the surgery was three in US dollars.

Episode Nine
Television

I loved to watch television. In Portugal, television was still only black and white at that time, and TV films were mostly imported from other countries and subtitled in Portuguese. Every Sunday afternoon, a Japanese animation drama for children called Heidi, the Girl of the Alps was shown, and I was excited to watch it because I could watch dogs and cats on this show. Marie and Chris used to watch mostly at night and I usually sat on one of their laps. I often watched together with them, but I couldn't understand the adult dramas, got bored, and fell asleep very quickly.

One night when I was sleeping peacefully on the lap of Marie, I was awakened by the sound of a woman screaming. When I looked around, I realized that the sound was coming from the TV — a woman was screaming and crying, crying and screaming! It sounded to me like something catastrophic had happened to her, or like the end of the world. As I moved closer to the TV screen in order to observe her more closely, I was reminded of the time when the butcher-doctor had neutered me. I thought perhaps the same thing had happened to her too, and I sympathized with her.

Episode Ten
Birthday

I turned one year old. I was growing bigger and bigger. By that time, I was growing long and looked like a dachshund dog, like a teenage human boy. The color of my eyes changed from grayish to golden yellow and they became round, big and bright; my short-hair coat turned smooth, shiny, silky and soft, like black velvet; my tail became longer and straight; my two ears stood sharply up in the air. I also had a high tone beautiful meowing-voice. I grew up to be a very handsome-looking cat, although I was not a fancy cat, I was simply a working-class-kitty.

A neighbor lady named Alexandra often used to visit Marie and Chris to talk about her husband who was in a jail as a political prisoner. She was deeply fond of me; she also had a Japanese name like me; her surname was Caimoto which was husband's family name. She questioned Marie why he had a Japanese name? Marie explained to her because her husband's ancestor was a Japanese way back four centuries ago, when Portugal and Japan were once trading allies, and some Japanese migrated to Portugal.

On the morning of my birthday, she appeared at our door holding a Portuguese fishcake with one candle on top of it. She looked at me saying, "Happy birthday, Kinoko!" It was a big surprise for me. I said to myself, "Is this the way humans celebrate their birthdays? Oh, I see! Am I joining the human's club, now?" As a birthday gift, she gave me a red handkerchief. "How pretty," Marie said, and put it on my neck straight away. I was not a communist cat but the red color was pretty and well matched to my black coat; I liked it very much. From that day on, I wore it around my neck every day for years until it fell to pieces.

Episode Eleven
Guests

While Marie was a good cat-food chef, Chris was a good human-food chef. Both of them loved cooking and invited their journalist colleagues for dinners almost every night, and many people would come and go from my home. The guests were mostly British, Americans, Canadians, Australians and Japanese. They came to visit Chris to get fast information about the revolution. Chris used to call them visiting firemen.

Most of the guests patted my head saying, "Your name is Kinoko? What a lovely name you have! It's cute!" But every Japanese guest said, "You name is Kinoko? What a funny name you have!" and laughed at me, because it's the name of vegetable in Japanese. It was little confusing for me — which comments should I believe!?!?

While they were dining, boozing, joking, laughing, smoking, and having a good time until the late evening hours, I used to sit quietly under the dinner table. There were many legs and shoes there. I knew which legs and whose shoes belonged to, because some guests wore the same old dirty shoes every time. It seemed to me that these guests never cleaned their shoes for years.

Episode Twelve
Paranoia

Meanwhile, Portugal's political situation changed its direction. Since the beginning of the revolution, Portuguese people had formed hundreds of political parties and organized hundreds of rallies. Among them was the Portuguese Communist Party (its abbreviation was PCP, same as my Portuguese Cat Party). The streets of Lisbon were colorfully decorated with red posters, red banners and red people were all over, and their political furor intensified over time.

One night, Chris came home in a panic and told Marie, "The Commies may take over Portugal! If this happens, military tanks will be in the streets, there will be a curfew, and all foreign journalists will be kicked out of the country. If this happens, it's going to be very quick, within hours of notice!" Marie also panicked. They discussed what they should do in such time of emergency. If Chris was expelled, he would fly to London, and Marie would stay behind, pack things up, and later join him.

While they were having this serious discussion, they never mentioned my name, they never said my name even once -- "Kinoko" or "Pugo". Both were so panicked that they completely forgot about me. I thought "I would be left alone in Portugal? I might become a homeless cat and have to live in the streets of Lisbon? What should I do?" My anxiety had begun...

Episode Thriteen
A Strange Phenomenon

Soon after, there was an important communist rally in a northern region in Portugal, and Marie and Chris were assigned to report on this; they left home very quickly. I was left alone in the apartment for the first time since being adopted. Alexandra came to feed me twice a day and played with me, but she never stayed with me overnight. During the days I stayed in the balcony, watching all sorts of activities in the streets — a farmer's market, chatting housewives, children playing, automobiles, motorcycles, and communists were marching with red banners. But during the nights, I missed Marie and Chris tremendously, believing they would never come back to me anymore.

When they returned ten days later, they noticed that my hair color had changed — my black coat had become a patchwork of black and white hair appearing all over my body — it was like salt & pepper. "What happened to Kinoko?" Marie wondered. Chris said, "Kinoko is getting old, you know!!!" "But he's only one year old, how come???" She questioned that I may become a white cat because my biological mother was white and my brother was black & white. I didn't know why such a strange phenomenon had happened to me. But day by day, the white hair gradually disappeared.

Marie guessed the change in my coat could be a psychological reaction: perhaps worrisome — I was worrying too much, thinking that Chris and Marie might have abandoned me and never return home: I would never see them again! This episode let Marie to believe, I had *thoughts and emotions*, even as a cat!

Episode Fourteen
Big Birds

Watching the streets from the balcony was an entertainment that I very much enjoyed. I was also able to take in the fresh air and bask in the sunshine of Portugal. Next to the balcony, there were big tall trees in which birds would sing and fly. It was fascinating to watch them; I could watch them for hours. I wondered why I couldn't fly freely like them. I used to stand on top of the balcony's guardrail and try to catch them, but I failed each time; I needed very long paws or wings that could carry me. Eventually, I gave it up and just enjoyed bird watching the whole day long.

One day, I heard an awful sound in my ears. Then I saw an enormous bird I had never seen before. "Oh, Waooo! The sky in Lisbon is not big enough for that bird!" I thought. More and more of these huge birds kept coming day after day and hour after hour, and soon they flew by every ten minutes. Then I learned a new word for them — *airplane.* Airplanes were a form of transportation for humans, and these airplanes were carrying colonial Portuguese who were returning home from Angola and Mozambique as the revolution closed to an end.

At that time, watching them and hearing their big noise, I never thought that I would find myself in an airplane being carried out of Portugal to the country called the United States of America in the near future.

Episode Fifteen
Kinoko goes to America

The communist crisis was eventually over, and by the end of 1976, a new democratic Portugal was born. After that, many cities were back to normal, and long absent tourists returned to Portugal. For journalists, there was nothing much to report or photograph for the foreign press anymore. Marie and Chris were talking about to move to the United States, to its West Coast — to the city of San Francisco.

As they talked about their new plan to go to America day after day, I became depressed again worrying, "How about me? Are they going to abandon me? Are they going to put me in a cat orphanage? Are they going to tell me goodbye after having enjoyed being with me….?"

Then, I started hearing the words I wanted to hear in my ears. The dialogue sounded to me like this: "America… San Francisco… I… Pugo… You… airplane… visa… Kinoko… cat box…" Finally, they mentioned my name often this time! Then, Chris said to me joyfully, "Kinoko, you are coming to America with us!" Marie assured me saying, "Pugo, you're going to become an American cat, okay?" It was like a dream come true to me — it was the happiest moment in my life: "I am going to Americaaaa!!!"

Episode Sixteen
A visa for cat

Portugal had a special law for animals: anyone who takes animals out of the country needed written permission from the government. This written permission was practically a visa for animals. When Marie went to the government office to get the permission to bring me to America, the document she brought back stated that I must leave the country within 15 days after the visa was issued. Otherwise, it will expire.

Then Marie went to Lisbon Airport to find out about animal shipment conditions. She found out that there was no direct flight from Lisbon to San Francisco on which I could be shipped. I would have to fly on TWA (Trans World Airlines) via New York, and it takes at least two days to reach San Francisco.

Marie and Chris had to fly to London first to see their editors, and in England, any animals that enter England are quarantined for six months by law, even if they are only passing in transit to another country. So Marie and Chris made an arrangement with their cat-lover friend: he would take care of me until they arrived to the United States. After they settled in their friend's house in Oakland, California, he would ship me to them. But everything had to be done within 15 days.

Episode Seventeen
Kinoko arrives in New York

The day I was supposed to arrive at San Francisco, Marie phoned the TWA cargo department at the airport, but no cat had arrived yet from Lisbon. Wondering why, she called her friend in Lisbon. He told her that Kinoko had left Lisbon on time — he had been tranquilized but had definitely gone on board. The third day, as still no Kinoko arrived, Marie became worried and called the TWA cargo office at New York Airport. The cargo officer said to her, "We have hundreds of black cats arriving from Lisbon every day, you know!" It sounded like a mass migration of cats from Portugal! He was joking of course — what he meant was, "A black cat flying from Lisbon to the United States? We never heard of it! As anyone hardly ships animals to the United States from Portugal, Kinoko was a very rare case."

"Oh, dear! Kinoko is lost," Marie thought. The fourth day, she panicked and called the office clerk again. He said, "Don't worry, we'll find him. The cat named Kinoko from Portugal, right? ... One of a kind...!"

Episode Eighteen
The story of Kinoko's Journey

The next day, the cargo clerk called Marie from New York and said, "We found Kinoko. He left this morning and is on his way to San Francisco!" When I arrived at San Francisco Airport, Marie was anxiously waiting for me. The moment she saw my cat box came out of the conveyor, I could hear her voice calling me, "Kinoko!?" I hadn't seen her for two weeks. I screamed loudly, "MEOW, MEOW, MEOW! Yes, I'm here, HERE!" I was telling her how much I had missed her. Then on our way home I kept meowing, meowing, meowing, and never stopped meowing. I was telling her my side of the story of what had happened to me at the New York Airport.

I told her that, first of all, the Portuguese TWA cargo worker at Lisbon Airport was entirely responsible for this delay; because he labeled my cat box as [KINOKO — A LIVE BLACK DOG] and shipped me. He didn't understand English well; for him, "cat meant dog" and "dog meant cat." So when I arrived in New York, I was categorized as a DOG and sent to the dog section right away. I was surrounded by hundreds of different creatures called DOGS, can you imagine? Until that point I had never seen such noisy animals all my life. They watched me through my box window and kept barking at me all the time because I looked different. I was terrified and defenseless. These were days of my nightmare. The proof of my misadventure was still attached to my box — the WRONG LABEL - DOG!

Chapter Nineteen
Another Theory

Another theory can be considered, however. When I reached the American Immigration Customer's Office at the New York Airport, the officer asked me, "You came from Portugal, didn't you? Portugal had a revolution recently. Have you ever been a member of the "PCP" (the Portuguese Communist Party)?" I was honest. I answered him "YES", because I thought it was the "PCP" (the Portuguese Cat Party). I told him that not only did I belong to it, I was the founder of the party and proud of it. Then the officer panicked and said to me, "You are under custody. We can't let you into the United States!" And I was segregated to a different room for interrogation.

It took me three days to explain to the American authorities that "PCP" means "PCP." At that time they suspected anyone who came from Portugal of being a communist. They thought I was a communist cat! Then, I pondered, "Who are the communists?" They then questioned me asking, "What is your religion? What do you believe?" Because I like to eat, so I said, "FOOD! I worship food and food is my religion!" After days of interrogation, I became frustrated because they were repeating the same questions. So I shouted at the officers saying, "MEAOOOO! " – "I am black, not RED!" They laughed at me and finally released me.

Episode Twenty
A House with Window by a Roof

Now, my new life in America had began. Until they found an apartment of their own in San Francisco, Marie and Chris were staying at the house of their couple-friend in Oakland, Todd and Linda, whom they had met in Lisbon. Their house was surrounded by trees and flowers in a quiet residential area. The penthouse bedroom in which we slept had a window connected to the roof, so that I was able to walk out onto the roof of the house, which was very exciting because we never had any windows in our Lisbon apartment — we only had a balcony. Every day I was out there taking the fresh air and enjoying "bird watching" again, as I used to do on the balcony in Lisbon.

The couple had a German shepherd named Oso (which means bear in Spanish; his face looked like bear). He was still a puppy and younger than me, but already big. While I was in custody at New York Airport, I saw many types of dogs, so that when I saw him I thought, "Huh, you again!" Dog was not a big deal to me anymore, and we soon became good cat/dog buddy and playmates. I used to scratch his big nose while he was asleep and he didn't mind it. When he barked, it echoed awfully. He kept saying repeatedly only ONE, ONE, ONE, never said TWO!

One day, I invited him to come with me to the most exciting place of the house: the roof. He said, "Oh, no! I'm scared. I can't." So I told him, "What a coward! A big animal who barks loudly and a big eater like you, how chicken you are!" I used to look down on him from the roof. Oso looked up at me from the ground enviously. I felt like I was a super-cat!

Episode Twenty-One
Kinoko fell from a window

Weeks later Marie and Chris found an apartment on Nob Hill in San Francisco, and I was taken to it. It was on the fourth floor with a basement, and had one bedroom, a living room, a kitchen and a bathroom. The bedroom had large windows with a backyard view, and the living room had a small window looking down onto a concrete basement ground. There was a long hallway, which was the perfect length for me to go jogging. This was our new home in America for the three of us: a Portuguese immigrant cat, Marie and Chris.

On the first day we moved in, as always out of my cat-curiosity, I first walked around examining the new pad, but soon began running, jumping happily and jogging up and down the hallway. Days later, one afternoon, Marie was in the living room sitting by the window and sorting out luggage. I saw the window next to her was wide open. I thought, "It's the window, again! I can go out to the roof from there again, just like before!" Without thinking, I immediately rushed to it, passing in front of Marie, and dived out. The next second Marie screamed "Oh, NOOO!!!" After that, everything was toooo laaaate!!! There was no roof outside the window and I was in the air falling down to the hard concrete basement. <Ahaaaa!!! I'm dooooomed...!!! Ahaaaa!!!>

Episode Twenty-Two
Window Phobia

After I hit the ground, I was still able to stand up, luckily. I was in a weird place; like I had landed on a different planet! I became terrified and almost fainted, and couldn't recall anything after that - I was trembling for fear. Shortly after with, Chris came down to rescue me. I wasn't harmed physically, but I was totally traumatized psychologically and for the next few days I grunted in fear and hid under the couch. I even didn't want to eat any food or to meow to Marie and Chris. I never forgot that "near dying experience" in my life.

    Because I had been moved one country to another and had experienced so many things in such a short period of time — leaving my Lisbon pad, staying at a friend's house, flying in an airplane, being held in "custody" at the New York Airport, exploring the roof in Oakland, and settling down in a new place in San Francisco — I was totally confused with these environmental changes about what was what and where was where. As a cat, I only have a tiny brain with which to operate my life. Honestly, I truly believed that every house in America had windows with access to an outside roof. After that suicidal experience I kept myself away from all windows: I developed a "window phobia."

Episode Twenty-Three
Fast-food for cats

As always, in my new home, the best place for me was the kitchen – kitchen was my "living room". And as always, Chris was in the kitchen cooking, and as always, I hung around with him while he was cooking. He was very generous; he used to give me all sorts of human snacks. He even sang songs for me calling me "Poogle, Woogle, Choogle, Noogle" and at the same time he enjoyed feeding me. When I meowed, for him it meant I wanted to eat. And, I was not even hungry, but every time I meowed, food came to me. So I kept eating.

One day he came back from the supermarket and said to me, "Kinoko, I have a very special gift for you. You've never had this before!" He showed me a colorful box with a picture of a ginger cat on it—the most famous American cat-star Morris. The box contained tiny biscuits. He started throwing the biscuits in the air one by one asking me catch them, as dogs do. "What kind of game is this? Is he boozing again?" I thought. The biscuits were called cat-food, a commercial fast-food produced only for cats, not for human. I thought they tasted just fabulous. I instantly became addicted to it. I now learned that all American cats eat this fast-food.

Episode Twenty-four
Kinoko uses a human toilet

Now that I had developed a window-phobia, I found the pad without a balcony or a roof is boring. But very soon I discovered another interesting place: the human bathroom. In Lisbon, my litter box was placed on the balcony; therefore, I didn't know what humans do in the bathroom. Because we didn't have a balcony or any other outdoor place in the new apartment, my litter box was set next to the human toilet in the bathroom. I had to share the room with Marie and Chris, and the bathroom door was kept always open, so that I could do my "business" at any time.

Now, for the first time, I had the chance to "watch" what humans do in there and how do they do it. I found out that they do exactly the same thing that I do! I wanted to try using the toilet myself. I sat exactly the way that I had seen Chris and Marie sit — the way humans do, and I made a poop there. It was a bit awkward for me—I had a hard time keeping my balance, but I succeeded. However, afterwards, I couldn't figure out what the water was there for or what to do with it. I pondered, "Was it there to drink or to wash my paws with, or what else...?"

Episode Twenty-Five
The Hot shot

Then, a half of hour, I heard Marie and Chris arguing:

Marie: "You didn't flush the toilet!"

Chris: "Yes, I did."

Marie: "Are you sure?"

Chris: "Of course, I'm definitely sure I did!"

Marie: "How strange! We don't have anyone else here!?"

I wore a very good poker-face. I pretended it had nothing to do with me. The next day when I had to go, I used the toilet again. But, soon after, while I was sitting on it doing my business, Marie suddenly opened the door and showed up in the bathroom. She caught me in the "act!" She couldn't believe what she saw in her eyes! She was absolutely stunned and just stood there by the door speechlessly. She then called Chris. He said to her, "Get a camera, quickly, Marie!" She grabbed the camera and took photos of me. This was an invasion of my privacy! (Ref: see back page of the book)

After that, I repeatedly used the toilet. But the thing I still couldn't understand was how to flush the water. After I used the toilet I wanted to cover my poop with something, like I always do in the litter box. Because I had the nature of a cat, I couldn't walk away from it, otherwise it would be very rude if I didn't.

Episode Twenty-Six
Aftermath

The only thing available nearby that I could reach was the toilet paper. When I pulled on the roll, the paper came down, so I covered the toilet bowl with it. But the rolling never stopped, so I continued to pull on the paper until all of it had come down. And I made terrible messes on the floor: not all of the paper went to the bowl — some of it was scattered all over the floor.

Marie found my messes and became angry at me. She then changed the position of the toilet paper so that it faced in the opposite direction, hoping that I would not be able to pull it down anymore. But I still had to cover my poop after I used it; it was my responsibility. As I looked around for an alternative, I spotted a bath towel hanging above the roll of toilet paper. So I pulled that down. Then I stuffed it into the toilet bowl in order to cover my "thing." Believing that I had done a perfect job, how smart I was, and I left.

Minutes later, Marie angrily shouted at me, "Kinoko! What have you done now? Come here! I'll beat you up!" "Oh, NO!" I thought, and immediately went into hiding. Marie was very angry at me because she had to pick the towel up out of the toilet bowl and throw it away. However, I continued to stuff towels into the toilet bowl time after time and repeated it again, and she had to pick it up each time. Finally, she and Chris became impatient with this situation, partly because when their guests come to use the toilet; they wondered what was going on in the bathroom. Marie and Chris were embarrassed.

Episode Twenty-Seven
Kinoko's Official Portrait

In the end, Marie and Chris decided to keep the toilet lid closed, declaring the human toilet for humans and the cat toilet for cats. Eventually I went back to my own litter box. However, Marie thought the photo of me — "A cat that uses a human toilet" — was funny. My eyes were serious and the expression on my face was authentic. She thought she could use it in a good photo story for newspapers.

She contacted several editors of major tabloids, but they rejected it, saying, "We have lots of people sending us with this sort of photos, but we never publish them because the toilet is not a popular subject — it's rude, vulgar, and not a romantic subject for our readers." Marie thought America was the country of "Freedom of Expression" with capital letters of F and E, but editors can't deal with the realistic side of cat beings, not even the tabloids. "This is censorship!" she told me and said, "Traditionally, Americans have had a great sense of humor. What happened to them, there is no freedom of the press anymore!?

Anyway, Marie made greeting postcards of my photo sitting on the toilet and wrote my toilet story on them. After that, I had to autograph them with my PAW using a black ink pad. She mailed them out to her friends all over the world. The photo became a symbol of me for years. She named it as "Kinoko's Official Portrait!"

Episode Twenty-Eight
Kinoko's American Dream

Now, both Marie and Chris realized that I have a high IQ — I was smarter than other average cats. Another thing that Chris taught me after we came to America was "The United States Constitution for Immigrant Cats." He told me that everybody in this country is given an equal opportunity, including a cat like me, and everybody can live their own dream. Once he asked me, "What is your dream, Kinoko, everybody can have dream, even cat like you!?" I told him, "I'd like to be a cat-star; like Morris. He is my great American cat-hero. Like him, I want to be in cat-food commercial actor, and my final goal is Hollywood!"

To start with, I have a talent that the superstar Morris even did not have: I can use the human toilet. I wanted to be on TV news — *"The cat who uses the toilet."* I could perform in front of the camera and would give interviews:

Reporter would ask me, "Mr. Kinoko, what is your opinion on the human toilet?"

Kinoko: "Frankly speaking, the flushing knob is too heavy for me. It should be digitized and placed next to the seat, perhaps the shape of PAW mark on it, so that any cat can figure it out after using it. If humans could invent such a technique, I assure you it might sell very well on the market. Cat-lovers certainly would buy it."

Reporter: "What a great idea! Thank you very much for your advice, Mr. Kinoko!"

Kinoko: "My pleasure! Have a nice day, sir!"

Cameraman: "Mr. Kinoko, please smile for the audience!"

Episode Twenty-Nine
Toilet Cat Revolution

After that, my next move would be to cast myself in a video: "Kinoko's Toilet Guide — How to use a Toilet for Cats." It would be an instruction in which I demonstrate how to use the toilet step by step: how to hold the seat correctly, how to keep one's balance, and how not to fall into the bowl, and so on. I could give a lecture from beginning to end in the video screen for the cat audience.

Cleaning the litter box is a headache for all cat-owners. However, showing the video would be an educational program for all American cats and it's a sensational idea too! If other cats could learn from me and begin using the toilet, they could resolve their messy litter problem — absolutely! Not only that, this could bring a *"Toilet Cat Revolution"* among all American cats and make my video a bestseller.

If these dreams become a reality, Marie will become my manager and Chris will be my promoter; he could write an article of me for newspaper. America is a "dream comes true-country. How many dreams one has, dreaming is always free, that includes cat like me!

Episode Thirty
Family Separation

After years of happily living with my human-parents, my destiny changed — Marie and Chris decided to live separately. It was sad time for me. The fact that I was able to develop such a unique "cat-nality" was the result of living with both of them. But now I had to choose one out of the two. It was a difficult decision for me. To be honest, Chris had been a good human-daddy for me: he fed me gourmet snacks and educated me on how to become a good American cat-citizen. On the other hand, Marie took care of my litter so that I had always enjoyed a clean litter box.

Without my consent however, Chris made a decision: "Kinoko is going to stay here with me," he told Marie. But Marie, of course, also wanted to live with me: I became their "custody battle." This created a situation — if I lived with Chris, Marie might come to "cat-nap" me, and if I lived with Marie, Chris might come to "cat-nap" me too. Whichever parent got me, I was destined to be abducted by "cat-snatcher", both of them anyway.

Marie soon found an apartment — luckily in the same block as our old pad. After months of custody negotiation, Marie won the case; I was taken to her place. However, there were special conditions: Chris had an "exclusive visiting rights" to come to see me occasionally, and he agreed to pay half of my medical bills every time I see doctors.

Episode Thirty-One
Meeting with Louis

The new apartment had two bedrooms, so Marie decided to have a roommate. A man named Louis moved in to live with us: he was a tall, charming and outstandingly good-looking guy who introduced himself a classical song singer. Because he wanted to become my roommate, I was entitled to interview him too. Marie introduced me to him saying, "----Kinoko---Pugo---Portugal--toilet: (His name is Kinoko; his nickname is Pugo. He was born in Portugal. He can use a human toilet.)

My first question to Louis was, "Do you cook? Are you a good cook?" Then I heard him telling Marie, "Besides singing, cooking is my greatest joy." I was very excited, hoping he'd be my new chef, and I welcomed him. He moved in with a big piano, music books, hundreds of cook books, and a lot of cooking equipment.

In his room, Louis set up a long vertical mirror in order to see his own facial expressions and body gestures to determine how he looked on stage while he sang. Every time I walked into his room, I could also see my own face in the mirror. Whenever he saw me, he used to greet me, "Hi, Pugo!" I used to watch his face from where I sat on the floor. To me, it seemed as though he was talking to his reflection in the mirror — he seemed to be thinking, "How good-looking I am!!!"

Episode Thirty-Two
Crime and Punishment

After Louis came to live in my place, my favorite kitchen became like a fiesta every day: Louis cooked meals three times a day and all sorts of food were scattered everywhere. Seated on a kitchen chair, I watched him cooking. He was a great cook indeed: he cooked artistically and elegantly. However, despite my great expectations, he never gave me anything — NO SNACKS for me. Having been raised on human food, it was very painful for me. I couldn't change my habits overnight just because a new man had moved in.

One day, as usual, when he prepared his lunch and was about to eat it, his phone rang. He rushed to his room leaving a piece of fish on the kitchen table. Now, my most favorite goody was sitting alone in front of my eyes. While he was talking on the phone I asked myself, "Shall I do it or not, that's the question?" The fish was very inviting and irresistible. Next moment, without thinking of consequence, I quickly snatched it and swallowed it to my mouth very quickly. When he returned to the kitchen, the fish had gone to my belly. I assumed a poker-face around him, but it didn't work on him. "Pugo! You did it, didn't you?" He suspected me immediately!

Then I heard him angrily complaining to Marie: "Pugo stole my lunch! You should educate him to American ways — NO SNACKS for the cat, okay?" Marie was embarrassed. She didn't beat me — instead, she locked me in a closet for hours. For the crime I committed, the punishment was a hard one.

Episode Thirty-Three
Birth of *Chanticleer*

Every morning at seven o'clock, before I got up, Louis began his voice lessons with a song by Schubert called Die Schöne Müllerin (The Beautiful Miller's Wife) — instead of 'Mostly Mozart' he was 'Simply Schubert.' His beautiful songs soon became my morning lullaby. Having sensitive ears to all kinds of sounds, listening to his voice, I began to feel the sound of the human mind and its emotions, and I started to figure out how he could do such a thing by voice. Out of curiosity, I began expressing "cat feeling" and "cat mind" through my "meow." Then I meowed in different tones — MeoO! mEow! meow! meeeooww! meoWWW! If I become a catsinger and could sing sitting on the toilet seat, my dream would come true fast — I'd be in Hollywood straight away.

Soon after, Louis established his own singing group called *Chanticleer* — an all-male a Capella choir which specializes in Renaissance and medieval era songs. Many young singers were in and out from my pad all the time. Because they were still unknown to the public and struggling financially, every singer had more than one job. Louis was singing at the Grace Cathedral and San Francisco Symphony Chorus while forming his own choir. As a cat-witness I can testify that Louis struggled for his dream — a music career. In the very beginning, its rehearsals were performed at my place, and believe it or not, I was the first and the only audience at that time.

Episode Thiry-Four
Snack Life Again

Marie decided to make a long trip overseas. I was taken back to Chris to live with him again until she returned. I became a rent-a-cat. Chris was very delighted and excited to live with me again. I was back to my old lifestyle: a snack life again. I was eating cats' fast-food for my main course, but also snack in between meals. The snack menu included fish, meat, kidney, liver, chicken, crab meat, prawn, cheese, sushi, and I ate vegetables as well: boiled potatoes, carrots, green peas, sweet corns, mushrooms (kinoko in Japanese), onions, spinach, tofu, nori, etc., I ate all kinds of human food, except garlic: only thing I didn't like was a 'garlic'.

After living with Louis, I had become an amateur cat-singer. I could "sing" in different intonations — voice up'n down, long'n short, high'n low, thin'n thick, soft'n hard; these skills I learned while listening to him. I had a high-tone meowing voice — I was a tenor. So, at Chris' place I was always "meowing," giving me 'voice lessons' just as Louis did in the morning. However, Chris never understood my voice talent. He thought I was asking for food every time I meowed. I ate his cuisine with more enjoyment than anybody else. He was very pleased and proud of his cuisine, and enjoyed feeding me many times every day.

Episode Thirty-Five
Kinoko Becomes a Fat-Cat

There are many ways to express a cat's feelings:
    Purring - I'm pleased; do some more.
    mEow means - I'm happy; nothing to complain about.
    MEow means - What are you doing? Can I join you?
    Me-ow means - I feel alone; I want to play.
    Me-o-wo means - I'm getting bored; want to do something.
    MeOww means - My litter is dirty; you must clean it!
    MWOW means – I'm angry; don't touch me!
    MEoww means - I don't like you; go away!
    MEOWWW means – I'm hungry; give me food!
    GIAOOO means — I'm in pain; help me someone!

By the inflections of our speech, human beings should be able to determine how cats feel. But Chris never got my messages. No matter what I told him, he always gave me food. By the time Marie returned, three months later, I weighed 21 pounds. She was very shocked because I didn't look like the "Kinoko" or "Pugo" I used to be. I looked like a monster-cat perfect for Halloween night. It was a terrible "cat-astrophe" for my career, because I was so heavy that I couldn't balance myself on the toilet seat anymore. This ended my hopes I had for my future dream —Hollywood.

Episode Thrity-Six
Diet

When Marie took me home, she laid a "diet" down on me. She thought that if I kept all that weight I might get a heart-attack and would die soon. Jogging down the hallway was just simply not enough exercise. From that day on, snacks were strictly prohibited. She bought Science Diet dry food and drastically eliminated the amount, giving me a small cup of the dry food twice a day — at 9:00 am and 5:30 pm. — with water, but nothing more.

I was hungry all the time, even right after the meal. I wanted to eat more. I kept meowing and begging for food the whole day long every day. Every time Marie went to the kitchen, I followed her shouting, "MEOWWW, MEOWWW", and demanded that she should open the fridge door screaming, "Give me food! Give me food!" Marie would say, "Kinoko, you just finished breakfast. Your belly clock is ticking too fast!" As she walked away from the kitchen without giving me any food, I would grab her feet from behind.

Marie occasionally takes a nap and while laying on bed and her eyes were closed, I didn't bother her, I kept quiet. But as soon as she wakes up and opened her eyes, I began meowing immediately and demanded food. Eventually, she couldn't stand with me anymore, a madly-screaming-cat; she stayed out of the apartment every day until 5:30 pm, my dinner time. It took me two long years to lose extra pounds. It was really a bloody tough hardship for me.

Episode Thirty-Seven
Birthday Party

On the 12th of February, 1985, I turned ten years old. Marie thought that it was a significant day for me: a Portuguese kitty that was living happily in America. So, she threw a big party for me inviting all of my cat-craze human buddies I've known since I came to America — it was an event intended especially for "Kinoko lovers only." My human guests were namely Chris, Todd, Bonita, Anna and Tim; no cat guest, only humans. Marie baked a cheesecake for me — my favorite goody! She put the flags of Portugal, America and Japan (because my name is Japanese) on top of it with candles.

When Marie lit ten candles on the cake, it was beautiful! My guests were all smiling at me and singing a birthday song for me: "Happy Birthday, Kinoko! Happy Birthday, Kinoko!" Then the cake was cut, and I was to eat the first piece in front of everybody. After I finished eating it, Tim asked me, "Have some more, Pugo?" And I ate the second piece, too.

It was a bit odd for me because I was "strictly prohibited" from eating any human food anymore, but now suddenly I was even being allowed to eat a dessert while a dozen smiling eyes were watching me. Although it's a human tradition, I couldn't understand exactly what was going on. Anyway, I enjoyed the cake — it was delicious! Life is wonderful; I wished everyday would be my birthday!!!

Episode Thirty-Eight
Meeting with a Professional Pet

One day, Marie came home carrying a box and said to me, "Kinoko, I have a special surprise gift for you!" I saw a creature coming out of the box, it had four legs like me! Marie said, "Her name is Mocha. She is your girlfriend, okay?" Being surrounded by only humans, I completely forgot about my own genetic roots. When I saw Mocha, I suddenly realized that I belong to a domestic animal called "CAT!" Mocha is a tiny female Siamese aged 16. Marie adopted her from her friend Ron. I and Mocha greeted each other telepathically saying:

Mocha: "You have an accent when you meow. Where did you come from?"

Kinoko: "I'm from Lisbon; I am a Portuguese immigrant cat. How about you?"

Mocha: "I'm from Pacific Heights, the most luxurious fat-cat district in San Francisco. I have blue eyes and blonde hair: I'm a fancy cat, a perfect pussycat-pet!!!

Kinoko: "But you have "crossed-eyed" called Lon-Pari (one looks at London and the other looks at Paris).

Mocha: "Because I'm a pure Siamese. Pure Siamese have Lon-Pari eyes by breed."

Kinoko: "You have shabby hair, look like a punk!"

Mocha: "Well, because of my age; I need a plastic surgery. But I'm tiny and look so young that I can lie of my age to humans as 16 months old! They believe me, you know!"

Kinoko: "Really!? Anyway, why are you here?"

Mocha: "This is my new home now. I'd like to be your "bride". Marie is our matchmaker. Do you like me?"

Kinoko: "You must be joking! You're old enough to be my grandmother!!!"

Episode Thrity-Nine
Mocha's Adventure

Marie was concerned about my lifestyle; I was surrounded by only humans since I was a kitten: eating human food, using the human toilet, meowing human songs, having human's birthday parties, and sleeping on a human-bed with Marie -- I was "too humanized" and forgetting my own roots. Mocha was here to "cat-nize" me.

Soon after, Mocha developed an adventurous talent. She loved to go out to the streets as dogs do. Since she was from an upper-class upbringing and lived in a mansion like a "queen", she was gorgeous, gracious and a great cat-host for the parties that Ron used to throw, and never afraid of strangers; she was a very much outgoing cat. Marie wrapped her up in a towel and carried her in her arms to nearby supermarket, stores, coffee shops, etc. I wasn't as talented as her, except for the toilet, and admired her courage. After Mocha and Marie came home, I asked Mocha what she had seen in the streets.

Mocha: "We went to Polk Street and I got a lot of attention from all sorts of people. Because I look so young and elegant that all cat-lovers just adored me saying, "What a cute cat!" and everybody said, "I wish my cat would be adventurous like you, Mocha!"

Kinoko: "Tell me about famous Polk Street, Mocha!"

Mocha: "I saw all different kinds of "queens" all over, so-called transvestites, you know? I wasn't the only queen! One of them asked Marie about my age. She responded, "How old do you think she is?" The "queen" said, "Sixteen years old!" When Marie questioned how can you tell, he replied, "Because I work at a cat-clinic!"

Kinoko: "Oh well, Mocha! Everybody gets old, not only you. I too will be old one day, same as all humans do."

Episode Forty
American Cat Family

I never knew that I was a "cat" until I met Mocha. To be honest, I've always thought of myself as a human, even I have four legs and humans have two legs. Mocha was also a cat who had a lot of experiences, and I was fascinated to learn about her life-story — a family life of American-cat. She became my cat-mentor.

Kinoko: "Have you ever had any children, Mocha?"

Mocha: "Oh, yes! When I was young and attractive. I have a husky voice that it sounds very sexy when I meow, so all males fell in love with me instantly. I once produced three kittens: all blue-eyed-blond-hair. They were beautiful, just like me! I have good genes. My genes will be a great heritage for America's future cat-generations. How about you?

Kinoko: "When I came to America, the out-of-wedlock lifestyle was an American institution and the population was rapidly expanding, including that of the cats. But I support a moral quality of life, and offspring should be raised in a traditional American-warm-family-home. Can, you agree with me?"

Mocha: "Oh, sure! My kids had never been beaten, abused, abandoned, abducted, and never lived in fear or violent, so they had healthy minds. I educated them very well, including how to use a litter box correctly. They all became good patriotic-cat-citizens! I'm very proud of them. I was a role model mother-cat!"

Episode Forty-One
Spoiled Cat-Roomate

Mocha's private life was a different story, however. Since she had become my lady cat-mate I had to share the litter box with her. The thing I found out about Mocha was that she had a "weird" litter habit: she never covered the "things" after she did it. Every time I went to use the box, "it" was still there. She had the worst toilet manners of any cat. This is not romantic at all. I complained to her:

Kinoko: "You didn't flush the toilet, Mocha!"

Mocha: "??? What are you talking about? I would never do such a thing!"

Kinoko: "What? You didn't learn about this from your biological-mother when you were a kitten?"

Mocha: "Well, yes, I did. I even taught my own kids the toilet etiquette. But in my youth I was very beautiful; I was called "Miss Pacific Heights" and had "queen's lifestyle," as you know. I was a perfect-pussycat-pet and everybody was fond of me, so I'm very spoiled. My fat-cat human-daddy was my servant: he did it for me. So I've forgotten how to do it now!"

Kinoko: "But you have to share the box with me now. I'm not going to do it for you, okay?"

Mocha: "I'm sorry for the inconvenience. I can't change my habits overnight just because I came here. I'll try my best, okay?"

Episode Forty-Two
Kinoko Goes on Strike

Despite my complaints, Mocha never did what I asked. I really hated to share the litter box with her uncovered "stuff." It was common sense for any cats to cover it, but she was a lazy-lady. On other hand, since she was so old, I thought I might be dealing with a cat that had "Alzheimer's disease." Maybe, that's why she was so forgetful.

I had to complain to Marie this time telling her, " Meoow (litter), meowww (stink), meeoow (disgusting)!" But she didn't get my message; she ignored what I was trying to tell her. Eventually I went on strike! There was a toilet rug next to the litter box and I did "it" on it. Then I folded up the rug and pushed it into a corner of the bathroom. Little after, Marie saw it and wondered why the rug was in disarray. When she discovered what I had done, she got mad like hell and chased me down, caught me, and beaten me savagely. I screamed madly like hell but, at least, she got my message regarding Mocha's terrible litter manner. In the end, she bought a new litter box for me— my own private use — and Mocha continued to use the old one. My strike had worked and I had won. I felt greaaat!!!

After living with me for ten months, sadly, Mocha passed away; she died. Poor Mocha! I felt a little guilty for her thinking that she might have committed suicide, because I stubbornly refused her marriage proposal — like the story of aging Cleopatra.

Episode Forty-Three
The Will

When I turned 14, concerned about my age, Marie made a Will for me. I was eating very well, playing well, sleeping well, and getting plenty of Californian sunshine. I was still in excellent health. But she was worried that I might live longer than her. In case she died before me, she decided to leave a Will for me. It stated; *"Any cat-lover who is willing to take care of my cat named Kinoko — an aging Portuguese Immigrant Cat — until his death. In return, you will receive $5,000 dollars' worth value of my camera equipments. This is written by Marie Ueda, the owner of Kinoko."*

However, before that happened, I had to approve my new owner to be. I had to interview and examine an applicant's personal resume to determine what sort of "cat career" he or she had established. For example, how many family members at his/her home, is there any dogs or cats living with them, is there animal "abuser" living there, what kind of food they would feed me, who would clean my litter box, and so on. There are crooks that pretend to be cat-lovers out of greed; I had to know those matters in advance, because I don't want to be adopted by wrong humans. In fact, I needed an attorney to protect Marie's Will.

Episode Forty-Four
Vacuum Cleaner

I hated the sound of the vacuum cleaner. It was too loud and noisy, and bothered my sensitive ears -- it sounded like a bulldozer to me. When Marie vacuumed the floor, I used to run away as fast as I could and hide myself in the closet or under the bed. But one day I didn't mind it at all: I was not afraid of it anymore. Marie praised me saying, "You have become brave, Kinoko! You finally are a strong machocat now. Very good!" and she began vacuuming my coat as well". At first I felt weird, but I soon felt comfortable, and after a few more times, I like it very much better than being handbrushed. After that, every time Marie vacuumed the floor, I was also "included in the job."

    Shortly thereafter I was taken to a doctor for a regular health check. The doctor discovered that one of my ears was losing its ability to hear: it was deaf. No wonder I couldn't hear very well and wasn't afraid of the sound of the vacuum cleaner: it didn't too loud anymore. Anyway, I loved having my coat massaged by the machine, so I kept having it done to me with the vacuum cleaner in the years following.

Episode Forty-Five
Kinoko Fell Ill

Marie had to make a long trip overseas; this time she had to be in West Berlin, then West Germany. I needed someone who could live with me and take care of me until she returned. Dozens of candidates came to see me. Because I was the one who lives with, Marie assigned me to the interview and directed me to choose one of them. After examining them telepathically through their eyes, I chose a woman named Violet. I told Marie, "I know she is a genuine cat-lover. I want to live with her."

Ten days after Marie left for Germany, I began to feel a pain in my face; it hurt so badly I meowed for days and nights. Wondering why I was crying, Violet looked at my face and found a tiny tumor on my right eyelid. She immediately took me to a clinic. I was diagnosed as having skin cancer, and hospitalized right away. The doctor said that for a cat to have this type of cancer is 'extremely rare': it's common for dogs, but not for cats. I had taken too many Californian sunbaths, perhaps. Anyway, as a skin cancer cat, I was the "second case" ever recorded in the entire the United States.

Violet notified Marie in Berlin. She was shocked by the horrible news of me and started crying — she called all of my human buddies in San Francisco making long distance calls, in order to tell them about me. Many of these friends showed up at my clinic to visit me — besides Violet, they were: Bonita, Chris, Denise, Louis, Elgy, Todd, and others. I was like a celebrity. The clinic had so much traffic from my visitors that the staff had to turn them away in the end.

Episode Forty-Six
Kinoko On The Phone

After being released from the clinic I was placed in intensive care. Since Violet couldn't be with me always, I was taken to Todd's place because he stayed home a lot and was available to take care of me days and nights. I was given painkiller pills but was constantly in pain and meowing 24 hours a day. Todd couldn't sleep during the nights. Despite all the trouble, I never lost my appetite; I was still eating very well because even though I was very sick. Todd was convinced that the days of my life were numbered and gave me plenty of food day after day. So I kept eating a lot of food.

Marie called Todd from Berlin almost every day. When she called, Todd put the phone to my ear so I was able to hear Marie's voice. She repeatedly said to me, "Hello, Kinoko! Are you there? Pugo! Are you okay?" I murmured, "Meoowww" — "The doctor said my days are numbered, but I can't believe him, because I still have an endless appetite!"

For my last days, I was taken back to my home again to be with Violet. Shortly thereafter while she was away from home, I walked to the kitchen, tried to eat my food, and I collapsed on the floor: I died in front of my own food and then fell into deep sleep forever. After that I have no earthly memory at all.

Episode Forty-Seven
Kinoko Goes to Heaven

When I woke up I was hovering at a gate made of rainbow. "Upon which planet did I arrive?" I thought. Then I saw someone waving at me. I wondered, "Do I know someone here?" When I looked at this creature closely, it was Mocha, my cat-lady-roommate who died years before me; I quickly recognized her by her Lon-Pari eyes. She was calling me, "Kinoko, come here this way! Join me!" I was warmly welcomed by her and we joyfully united together. The most beautiful part of my life-story is that I've since married to Mocha in Heaven!

We became the most lovable cat-couple in eternal life; it's a honeymoon forever. There is no food, no litter, no kitchen here and nobody meows, either. It's totally world of silence; we have only spirits and souls, and it's beautiful. This is a "life-after-death" for cats! Nothing else to do here except cat-chats. Mocha and I chatted our lifetime memoirs: my good old days in Portugal, my journey to America, Mocha's glorious days in Pacific Heights, and we laugh about her toilet manner and my toilet story, etc. We chatted about a lot of things.

Kinoko: "Life as a cat is the easiest living of all. It's better than being human! This is because being good-pussy means being selfish, self-centered, snobbish, arrogant, aloof, uncompromising, obstinate and mysterious. People love us and those cat-crazes are everywhere. Humans are funny animals, aren't they? Anyway, we had the best privileged life and I enjoyed my life tremendously!"

Mocha: "So would you like to be reborn as a cat" Kinoko?"

Kinoko: "Oh yeah, absolutely! I'll be a "Born-Again-Cat," of course!!!"

Episode Forty-Eight
Soul mates

Some years later, guess who showed up?! — "Louis," the founder of Chanticleer who died years after me. He said, "Hi, Pugo! Nice to see you again! Can I join you?" He also remembered Mocha. It was a wonderful reunion for all of us and a chance for him to join our chat-club. In the eternal world, all ex-creatures become equal and we are able to chat spiritually in the same language. Louis, Mocha and I became soul mates.

    I apologized to Louis because I used to steal his food, you know: I was a naughty big-eater. After I died Marie used to tell him the story of how I died: I died in front of my own food in the kitchen. Louis would laugh at me how much I loved "eating." He used to joke that he also should die in the kitchen, same way I did because he loved "cooking" so much. Louis told me that Marie had published a book about Germany, and that her next book is about me. Is she going to expose my privacy? He also said that before he came to Heaven, he said goodbye to everybody he knew: Marie, Chanticleer singers, and all others who used to come my home for rehearsal. Although I couldn't make my dream come true (the toilet story), but Louis did: his work of Chanticleer was a great contribution to American music world and should be remembered forever.

    Anyway, he congratulated me on my marriage to Mocha and sang wedding-songs for us. Louis is singing in Heaven too! His beautiful voice echoes all over Heaven, just like it used to echo in my home. We three are having a great after-life together!

Afterward by the Author

This has been a story of Kinoko-the Portuguese cat that had a Japanese name, migrated to America and died peacefully in San Francisco. He died on the first of December, 1990: he was almost 16 years old. I have a neighbor friend named Bonita. She is also a great cat-lover and a longtime friend of Kinoko. She has a beautiful garden in the backyard at her apartment, and a number of her cats were buried there. Some years ago I briefly mentioned to her that I would like Kinoko to be buried there, joining to her kitties in the garden. She remembered this. When Violet notified her that Kinoko's death, within hours she came over to my apartment and took over his body, carried it to her garden, and buried there. I was grateful to Bonita for her warm thoughtfulness. Bonita recalled, "The day Kinoko died, it was a dramatic sunset in the sky, a beautiful ending of the life for Kinoko!"

After I returned from Berlin, I visited Kinoko's grave. Ever since, I have visited the grave to give him flowers on his birthday and the date he died. One of such days, a funny coincidence occurred. Bonita and I saw mushrooms (Kinoko) growing in front of his grave. Kinoko could be sending me a message-hi, Marie! At first we laughed, but afterwards it crossed my mind, "Are cats spiritual? Do they have soul?" This convinces me YES they do. Perhaps, he was telling me, "I had had a wonderful life as a cat. Thanks, Marie, for not abandoned me in Lisbon and took me in to San Francisco. I truly enjoyed my American life; the United States is indeed a great country taking care of all immigrants, even cat like me: a third-class citizen. I was the luckiest immigrant-cat in the world! Many Thanks, Marie, I never forget you!!!"

About the Author

Marie Ueda is a Japanese-born photojournalist who worked for The Guardian newspaper of London, England. As a nonfiction author, she has written the following books: "Testimony of the Twentieth Century" – Before and After the Berlin Wall (1996); "Life is a Wonderful Experience" – Autobiography of a Photojournalist (2018) which was rated Five-Star at amazon. com; "PORTUGAL" — its history, people and the Carnation Revolution (2021); "JAPAN 1945" – Atomic Bomb, Emperor Hirohito and MacArthur (2022); "Life with the Wall": Berlin 1961-1989 (2022); "A Memoir of Chanticleer" — My life with Louis A. Botto (2022). Her website is: www.marie-ueda.com.

*Did you like my story...?
If you do, please name your next cat, Kinoko!
Thanks*

www.ingramcontent.com/pod-product-compliance
Ingram Content Group UK Ltd.
Pitfield, Milton Keynes, MK11 3LW, UK
UKHW022209230426
12048UKWH00016BA/737